RIDING
HALF-PIPES

rosen publishing's
rosen
central®

Published in 2017 by The Rosen Publishing Group, Inc.
29 East 21st Street, New York, NY 10010

Library of Congress Cataloging-in-Publication Data

Names: Michalski, Pete. | Hocking, Justin, author.
Title: Riding half-pipes / Peter Michalski and Justin Hocking.
Description: First Edition. | New York : Rosen Central, 2017. | Series:
  (Skateboarding Tips and Tricks) | Includes bibliographical references,
  webography and index.
Identifiers: LCCN 2016008904 | ISBN 9781477788806 (Library Bound) | ISBN
  9781477788783 (Paperback) | ISBN 9781477788790 (6-pack)
Subjects: LCSH: Skateboarding--Juvenile literature.
Classification: LCC GV859.8 .M54 2017 | DDC 796.22--dc23
LC record available at http://lccn.loc.gov/2016008904

Manufactured in China

CONTENTS

INTRODUCTION

You might remember the first time you saw a halfpipe and thought about one day getting up there to land exciting and seemingly effortless tricks. Getting on the halfpipe is a big reason many people start skating to begin with.

Halfpipes are seen on television coverage of skateboarding contests and demos, in all the skating games, and they exist all over, probably even in your local skatepark. If you are lucky, a friend or acquaintance might even have one in their backyard. You may be thinking of launching 15 feet (4.6 meters) in the air on it.

For many younger or inexperienced skaters, starting out on halfpipes might seem a bit intimidating at first. Even if you have a little bit of experience on them, learning better and more complicated tricks will take some time.

No matter what your skill level, this book should have something for you, from step-by-step instructions on the basics of riding halfpipes, to some more of those advanced tricks. With the helpful tips in here, and with a commitment to learning—and, most importantly, having fun—you will hopefully be ripping a halfpipe in no time. Grab your board and drop in!

Riding halfpipes is an integral part of the sport and culture of skateboarding throughout North America and worldwide. There is a particular set of skills—and thrills—that halfpipes offer that keeps ramp and vert skaters coming back.

CHAPTER ONE

WHY SKATERS LOVE HALFPIPES

Nowadays, skaters have so many options of where and how to skate. Years ago, street skating was the most popular simply because everyone had somewhere they could do it, while skateparks and halfpipes were more rare. While almost all amateur and pro skaters can appreciate the thrill and freedom of doing grinds and slides all over parking lots, office plazas, and off of benches and curbs, many of the same skaters will also rave about halfpipes.

In fact, many pro skaters may tell you that some of their most memorable skate sessions took place on a halfpipe. Why is this? Because there's an incredible sense of exhilaration you get from rolling on a halfpipe's smoothly curving surface, similar to the feeling a surfer gets from riding a perfect wave. And unlike a lot of street spots where you're more likely to get kicked out if you skate in a large group, halfpipes are a great place for a bigger crew of skaters to have fun and build their skills without coming into conflict with authorities and law enforcement.

HOW IS A HALFPIPE SET UP?

Before you hop on a halfpipe, it's important to know the names of all the different halfpipe elements. Most halfpipes are made of plywood and then surfaced with a smooth material called Masonite. Masonite wears out pretty quickly though, so newer, more weather-resistant surfaces like Skatelite, a plastic-based surface, are becoming popular.

The curved sections of the halfpipe are called transitions, trannys, or walls. Most halfpipes have two transitions facing one another, which can vary in size and steepness. The horizontal part of the halfpipe that sits just above the ground separating the two transitions is called the flat bottom. Most halfpipes have at least 12 feet (3.7 meters) of flat bottom, which gives you plenty of time to set up for tricks between walls.

At the top of each transition is a round metal pipe called the coping or the lip. The coping is a surface for doing grinds and stalls, and it helps you pop out (bounce your wheels off the coping for extra height) on aerial tricks.

Finally, sitting on top of each transition you'll find the decks. This is where skaters chill out in between runs.

Some halfpipes have added features that make them more fun and challenging to skate. Sometimes skaters want an extra few feet of height on the top of a small section of their halfpipe, so they'll add what's called an extension or a tombstone.

If the lip of an extension or tombstone angles down until it reaches the normal height of the halfpipe, this is called an escalator. Just like the escalator in the mall can take you from the second floor to the first floor, a halfpipe escalator allows you to grind smoothly from an extension down to the lower part of the halfpipe's lip.

Lizzie Armanto, one of the brightest new stars of modern skating, rides a halfpipe during a demonstration event at the 2015 World Extreme Games in Shanghai, China, on April 25, 2015.

A sloping passage that connects the deck to the transition, cutting away the lip, is called a roll-in or a channel.

A spine is where two complete halfpipes are set back to back, so that their copings are welded together at the top. This allows skaters to grind or air from one halfpipe to the other.

And a hip is created when two halfpipes are placed next to one another and at a slight angle. A hip also allows skaters to transfer from one halfpipe to the other.

CHOOSE YOUR WEAPON: MINI OR VERT?

Most halfpipes are unique in some way, but there are two main varieties: the mini (miniature) halfpipe and the vert (vertical) halfpipe. Mini halfpipes are a good place to learn basic tricks. They're usually somewhere between 2 feet (0.6 m) and 8 feet (2.4 m) tall, with transitions that are fairly easy to maneuver.

Vert halfpipes are much taller. They're usually between 9 and 13 feet (2.7 and 4 m) high. Vert halfpipes typically have about 9 feet (2.7 m) of transition, and at least 1 foot (0.3 m) of vertical at the top, just below the coping. This is why they're called "vert" halfpipes.

A skater performs a backside grind on a mini-ramp in this vintage photo captured in Goleta, California, in August 1987.

WOMEN: MAKING A MARK

There aren't as many female skaters as there are males. But young women often find that halfpipes are a good place to start developing basic balance and coordination on a skateboard. Some female professionals like Carabeth Burnside and Jen O'Brian have even made a whole career out of skating halfpipes.

Every day more and more girls are beginning to skate. So don't be shy. You can pick up some halfpipe basics in just a day or two, even if you're just starting out.

One skater who made her mark throughout the 2000s was Lyn-Z Adams Hawkins, hailing from Southern California. Hawkins won eight medals for vert at the Summer X Games throughout the decade (three gold, four silver, and one bronze), and was the first female to execute an aerial called the 540 McTwist.

Another famous female skater is Vanessa Torres. After Hawkins and Ellisa Steamer, the first documented female pro skater, Torres was the third woman to be a playable character in Tony Hawk's series of skating video games.

One skater who probably has a big future is Alana Smith, who at age 13 in 2013 became the youngest medalist (male or female) at an X Games ever.

HALFPIPE ETIQUETTE

Your parents taught you your manners, right? Skateboarders have manners, too, and there are some important ones you need to know about at halfpipes and public skateparks.

Manners are especially important on a halfpipe because they help keep you and others safe. Here's a list of the three most important manners you need to know about:

1. Watch and Learn: When you show up to a new halfpipe or skatepark, spend some time watching people skate before you even step on your own board. Pay attention to the way experienced skateboarders use the halfpipe, and watch to see what lines they take. Watching the masters will help you learn, and also help you avoid accidents and collisions.

2. Wait Your Turn: When skating a halfpipe, wait your turn, or else you might get called a snake. (A snake is someone who doesn't wait his or her turn and cuts other skaters off. It's definitely not cool to be a snake.) Never drop in a halfpipe in the middle of someone else's run on the halfpipe. And keep your board out of the drop-in position (the position where you place your trucks and wheels out on the coping) whenever someone else is skating.

3. Don't Hog the Halfpipe: If the halfpipe is crowded, don't spend too much time on one run. Make a few turns, and then let someone else go. Don't worry, you'll get plenty of time to skate.

SAFETY FIRST

So you're ready for a halfpipe session, right? Well . . . almost. You need to know just a couple more things about safety, and then you'll be good to go.

The height and steepness of halfpipes may seem intimidating at first, but you will probably be surprised how fast you get the hang of it. Be adventurous, but realistic.

When skating a halfpipe, it is important to wear reliable and durable knee and elbow pads (we'll talk more about how to use your pads in the next section).

Remember: Always skate at your own pace and skill level. It may be intimidating to be around a lot of skaters who are better than you. Don't feel pressured to try something you can't possibly do. It's not a competition, and everyone was just starting out once, just like you. Putting too much pressure on yourself can cloud your judgment, leading you to take risks that could land you in the hospital.

Think about how good it feels to learn a new trick, and the hard work and trial-and-error it takes to get there, even for just a basic maneuver. Take it slow, and you'll get to the harder stuff later. Thinking excessively about others' opinions of you will just rob the sport of any fun.

CHAPTER TWO

STARTING OUT

I t is very important that you wear kneepads and a helmet when you get on a halfpipe. It is a long way down, and the halfpipe itself is a solid object that can do a lot of damage with the help of gravity—a painful and even potentially fatal situation. TSG, Pro-Tec, 187, and a few other companies all make high quality pads, the kind with a thick plastic cap over the kneecap.

If you've seen lots of people skate a halfpipe, then you know exactly what this cap is for: when experienced skaters fall, instead of flopping like a dead fish to the bottom of the halfpipe, they drop to their knees and slide gracefully down the transition on their knee pads. Before you start actually skating a halfpipe, it's a good idea to practice some knee slides, and here's how:

TRICK:

1. Run a few feet up the transition of the halfpipe.
2. As you near the top of the halfpipe, turn around and fall to your knees.

While you will need safety equipment at all stages of your development as a halfpipe skater (or anywhere else you choose to board), it is especially important for beginners, who are more prone to falls.

3. Slide down the transition on your knee pads with your feet dragging beneath you. Place some weight on your feet beneath you, but avoid sitting down too hard on your heels, which could lead to an ankle or foot injury.

4. As you slide, lean back a little. If you start to fall forward, instead of putting your hands out in front of you and risking an arm or wrist injury, fall onto your elbow pads and use

them to slide, the same way you slide on your knee pads. It's sort of an awkward position, but you'll get used to it.

5. Once you've gotten the hang of this, try working your way higher up the halfpipe and doing longer slides. If you're practicing on a smaller halfpipe, you can also try a knee slide starting from the deck of the halfpipe.

PUMPING

Now it's time to learn the most basic element of skating halfpipes: pumping. Pumping is the action that keeps you moving on a halfpipe instead of slowly coming to a stop. It's what gives advanced skaters the momentum to take those long runs, linking trick after trick after trick. Just as you had to slowly learn how to walk long before you ever set foot on a skateboard, it's essential that you learn to pump before you learn how to drop in. Like learning how to walk, pumping feels a little weird at first. It's a completely new kind of movement, and it takes some getting used to.

Another important thing to know is that it's easier to pump on a slightly bigger halfpipe. The transitions on a bigger halfpipe are usually a little less steep, and you don't have to worry about hitting the coping once you start getting higher.

The secret to pumping is pressing down on your board as you skate up and down the transitions of the halfpipe. Pressing down on your board as you go up and as you come down each transition is sort of like pressing down on a gas pedal in a car. When you apply downward force with your legs and feet, you pick up speed (*major* speed if you push hard enough).

Keep in mind that the pumping motion comes all from your legs. So make sure to bend with your knees. And instead of hunching over too much, keep your waist pretty much straight up and down.

Riding halfpipes lets you get much higher than you normally would when doing tricks from a position on the ground. This is a major appeal of doing halfpipe tricks.

You can think of pumping as a sort of one-two rhythmic motion. You pump once as you go up each transition, and then you pump again as you come down, one-two, one-two. Here it is step-by-step:

TRICK:

1. Start off by standing on your board on the flat bottom.
2. Start pushing toward the opposite wall. As you put your back foot back on the board, make sure your feet are

aligned and that your weight is spread evenly over both feet. Your front foot should be directly above the mounting bolts for your front truck. Your back foot should sit in the pocket, the area where the tail of the board starts to angle up. Keep most of your weight on the balls of your feet, rather than having it all just on your toes or heels.

3. Approach the transition with your knees slightly bent. Once you reach the transition, use the energy in your bent knees to stand up a little bit while you press down on the skateboard as you move up the transition. Make sure to press down evenly with both feet.

4. Avoid leaning toward the wall as you travel up the transition. If anything, lean back a bit towards the flat bottom, so that your body remains perpendicular to the skateboard. As you travel up the wall, bend your knees again slightly.

5. As you begin to roll back down the transition, don't turn the skateboard. Simply turn your head in the direction you're moving and look where you're going. Remember that to get the most speed you need to pump as you come down, too. So press down on the board again as you roll back through the transition. Once you reach the flat bottom, you should be standing up straight again, ready to pump the next wall.

Keep working on pumping until you can get higher and higher and hold your speed in the halfpipe. It takes a while, but eventually you'll get it. Set small goals for yourself. For instance, you might pick out a sticker or a row of screw-heads toward the top of the halfpipe, and try to touch it with your front wheels. Once

VISUALIZING TRICKS

Ask any pro skater, and he or she will tell you that skateboarding takes just as much mental effort and imagination as it does physical skill. Before you try any new trick, picture yourself doing it in your head. Go through each motion as if you were watching yourself in a movie. See yourself landing the trick perfectly.

Imagine your foot position, how it will feel when you land, etc. Really see yourself riding away clean. If it helps, imagine very specific details like the color of your shirt and the sound of your friends cheering after you land.

Once you actually go for the trick, say to yourself "I can do this." Eventually you will. For a slight variation, imagine your favorite pro skater landing the trick, and then try to imitate his or her style.

you start getting close to the lip of the halfpipe, you're probably ready for the next step: dropping in.

DROPPING IN

Your first time dropping in can be a little scary, but it's also one of the most thrilling things you'll ever do on a skateboard. Now that you know how to pump, dropping in is really pretty simple, even though it might make your heart pound and your hands sweat the first time you try it. But before you learn any other tricks on a halfpipe, you have to drop in first. Starting

Dropping in is the best and primary way to gain the speed you need on a halfpipe. Make sure to know your turn. Coordinating with fellow skaters will prevent collisions and other mishaps.

from the top of the halfpipe is the only way to get enough speed to set up for other tricks. Here's how to do it:

TRICK:

1. Set your tail down on the coping of the halfpipe with the trucks and wheels hanging over the edge. Place your back foot on the tail to keep the board in place. Keep your knees bent slightly.

2. Slowly move your front foot forward, keeping most of your weight on your back foot. Rest your front foot at a slight forward angle over your front bolts, and keep your knees bent.

3. Now begin to lean forward, getting your hips out over the board and shifting much of your weight from your back foot to your front foot. Keep your shoulder tucked a little bit as you lean forward, and avoid the urge to lean backwards. As your hips begin to move forward, straighten your front leg out a little. Press down firmly with your front foot, pushing the nose of your board down into the halfpipe so that your front wheels make solid contact with the transition.

4. Keep your knees bent slightly and ride down to the flat bottom. Congratulations on your first drop in!

CHAPTER THREE

BASIC TRICKS ON THE HALFPIPE

After learning how to pump and drop in on a halfpipe, your next step is actually learning some basic tricks. Thus far, you can go forward and backward on the halfpipe, and probably not much else. It is time to learn how to move around and use the whole halfpipe.

KICK TURNS

The best way to do this is by learning how to turn the board with a trick called a kick turn. Most people start out learning backside kick turns, which means you turn toward the board in the direction of your toes (it's called backside because your back faces the coping of the halfpipe as you turn). Once you get the hang of going backside, try some frontside turns, or turns that are in the direction of your heels. It's the same motion, only you have to look over your lead shoulder as you turn. Here's how to do them:

TRICK:

1. Approach the transition with your knees slightly bent.

This skater seems to defy gravity itself while performing a backside kickturn.

2. As you reach the lip, lift up your back heel just slightly and press down on your tail with your toe. This helps you lift up your front trucks and wheels just slightly off the halfpipe surface.

3. With your lead shoulder slightly tucked, turn your lead hip and shoulder 180 degrees, until they're pointing in the direction of the opposite wall of the halfpipe. (For a backside kick turn, turn in the direction of your toes. For a frontside turn, turn in the direction of your heels.) You don't have to whip your body around here. Just let gravity pull your body and your board around as you set your wheels back down.

4. Pump the transition as you come back down and prepare for the next wall.

Kick turns are a great foundation trick, because once you get the hang of them, you'll have no problem doing some other simple tricks, especially grinds.

GRINDS

A simple backside grind is really nothing more than a kick turn, except you go a little higher on the halfpipe, so that when you turn, your back truck makes contact with the coping. Once you get a few backside grinds, try it frontside, too. Here's how:

TRICK:

1. Approach the wall at a slight angle, either backside or frontside, with enough speed to reach the lip of the halfpipe.

A skating instructor shows young students a frontside grind on a modified halfpipe, sometimes called a micro-quarterpipe.

2. As you start to make your kick turn, raise your back heel and use the toes on your back foot to put a little extra pressure on the edge of your tail. This makes it easier for your back wheel to lap, or ride over, the coping so your truck will grind the lip.
3. As your back truck hits the coping, shift some of your weight to your back foot. Make sure you lean forward as you grind and keep your body leaned into the halfpipe.
4. As you complete your grind, again put some pressure on the edge of your tail. This will help to get your back truck and wheel off the coping smoothly.
5. Keep your knees bent and ride down the wall.

DOING AXLE STALLS

Once you get the hang of simple grinds (some people call them scratcher grinds, because you're basically just scratching the coping), you can start thinking about axle stalls. "Axle" is another name for your trucks, so when you do an axle stall, you rest both trucks (along with your whole body) on the top of the coping, rather than grinding.

Axle stalls are another important foundation trick, and they lead to some of the intermediate tricks (like the 50-50) that we'll talk about in the next section. Here's how to do an axle stall.

TRICK:

1. For an axle stall, unlike a grind, you want to make a straight-line approach to the lip. You don't need to go at an angle because you won't be moving across the coping. You also need some extra speed to get all the way on top of the deck.

2. As you reach the top of the halfpipe, press down on your tail and lift up your front truck so that it doesn't hit the coping.
3. Set your back truck on the coping first, putting some extra weight on your back heel so you can get your board and body all the way up on the deck.
4. Once your back truck is resting on the coping, use it to pivot your shoulders and hips around so they're in line with the coping below you.
5. Set your front trucks down, keeping the weight on your heels and your body leaning in toward the halfpipe.
6. After you stall for a second, press down on your tail with the toes of your back foot, lean forward, turn off the coping, and ride back into the halfpipe.

TAIL STALLS

Another simple stall you can try is the tail stall, also called the tail tap. If you can drop in and pump, then tail stalls will come pretty naturally, because they involve the exact same motions as dropping in.

Like axle stalls, tail stalls are a good set up trick. It gives you a chance to get set for more difficult tricks. While the goal with a tail stall is to ride up backwards, set your tail down on the coping, and then rest for a second on the lip, you can work your way up by tapping your tail below the coping (on the halfpipe surface) a few times, just for practice. Here's how to do the tail stall:

TRICK:

1. Approach the wall going backward (riding backward is also called going fakie) with enough speed to reach the lip.

2. As you approach the coping, bend your knees and press down on your tail with the ball of your foot.

3. Straighten out your back leg, jamming your tail up on to the coping and the deck. As your back leg straightens out, your front knee should bend up towards your torso.

4. Stall on your tail for just a second, getting your body all the way up on the deck.

5. Now straighten out your front leg and press down on your front foot, just like dropping in!

PLAYING "ADD-A-TRICK"

Once you get a few intermediate and advanced tricks under your belt, you're ready to play a famous skate game called Add-a-Trick. First, get at least three friends of equal or similar skate ability together. Then decide on a designated order to skate in, so that the same person always goes first, second, third, and so on.

To begin the game, the first skater drops in and does a trick. The next skater has to do that trick, and also add another trick. The skater after that has to do the first two tricks, and add a trick of his or her own, and so on. As soon as anyone misses one trick in the sequence, they're out. Things get pretty fun (and pretty hectic) after a few rounds, once you have to do five or more tricks in a row. The last person to complete the run and add a new trick, wins.

ROCK-AND-ROLL TO FAKIE

A good trick to do after you drop in from your tail stall, and another important basic trick, is the rock-and-roll to fakie. When you do a regular rock-and-roll, you jam your front trucks and wheels up over the coping and then turn backside into the halfpipe. But with a rock-and-roll to fakie, you come down the wall backward.

One good way to warm up for a rock-and-roll to fakie is by riding up the wall below the lip and lifting your front trucks and wheels slightly off the halfpipe, like you're doing a little manual, or a wheelie, just below the coping. Do a few of these manuals, working your way higher and higher. Once you can reach the lip, you're ready for the real thing.

A skater does a rock to fakie, with his front trucks and wheels over the coping.

TRICK:

1. Ride straight up the transition, leaning back just slightly.
2. As you approach the lip, press down on the tail with your back foot, lifting your front trucks and wheels over the coping.

3. Set the center of your board down on the coping by straightening out your front leg and using your foot to press your front truck and wheels down on the deck. At the same time, bend your back knee. These two motions combined will make your back wheels come off the halfpipe in a rocking (or teetering) motion.

Launching into the air is one of the main attractions of riding halfpipes.

4. As you stall, shift your weight to the outside edge of your back foot, so that the inside edge of your foot lifts up slightly. Use the outside edge to press down on the tail and lift your truck and wheels back over the coping.

5. Set your front trucks back down on the halfpipe, and shift some of your weight to your front foot. As you roll backwards down the halfpipe, turn your head and look directly towards the opposite wall.

INTERMEDIATE HALFPIPE TRICKS

You are probably getting antsy to attempt some harder tricks, now that you have had enough practice at basic ones like axle stalls and rock-and-rolls to fakies. Chances are you are gaining more confidence on the halfpipe itself, and going faster as a result. That's good. The next round of high-powered tricks need speed.

THE 50-50 GRIND

One trick that definitely takes a little more speed is the 50-50 grind. The 50-50 grind is an essential trick. It helps you get speed for highly advanced tricks like airs and inverts. A 50-50 grind involves almost the same motions as an axle stall, except you actually grind across the coping instead of just stalling. Here's how to pull it off:

TRICK:

1. Approach the coping as you would for an axle stall, except with more speed and at more of an angle.

This skater is executing a grind along the lip of of an indoor ramp, one of many moves that requires a good sense of balance.

2. Similar to when you're doing an axle stall, lift your front truck and begin grinding on your back truck. Once your back truck is firmly on the coping, set down your front truck.

3. As you grind on both trucks, put pressure on both your heels, so that you stay up on the deck. But, at the same time, keep your body weight and waist in toward the halfpipe so you don't roll out, and so you're ready to drop back in.

4. As you complete your grind, press down on your tail with the ball of your back foot, while turning your hips and shoulders back into the halfpipe.

5. Keep your knees bent slightly as you drop back in and head toward the opposite wall.

THE BOARDSLIDE

Just like 50-50s are an easy step up from the axle stall, the boardslide is just an advanced form of the rock-and-roll to fakie. Instead of just stalling, though, you actually slide across the coping on the bottom of your board.

This skater is executing a grind along the lip of of an indoor ramp, one of many moves that requires a good sense of balance.

TRICK:

1. Approach the wall as if you were going to do a rock-and-roll to fakie, except with much more speed and at more of an angle to the coping. The angle will give you the momentum to slide, rather than just stall.
2. Set the center of your board on the coping, put enough weight on your front foot so that your back wheels lift off the surface of the halfpipe, making it possible for you to slide.
3. Press down on the balls of your feet, making the center of your board slide across the coping.

4. As you near the end of the slide, lift up the inside edge of your back foot. Press down on the tail with the outside edge of you back foot, and lift your truck and wheels back over the coping.

5. When you set your front trucks and wheels back down on the halfpipe, put some extra weight on your front foot. Turn your head and look over your lead shoulder as you roll backwards toward the flat bottom. Keep your knees bent to absorb your weight as you hit the transition.

After these basic grinds and slides, you're probably getting the natural urge to go above and beyond the coping. Halfpipes are the best place for doing airs; world records for the highest airs were set on halfpipes. But before you start going head-high, you have to learn the basis for all airs: the ollie.

The ollie—shown executed here—is one of the most common skate maneuvers, and translates well from the ground to halfpipes.

THE OLLIE

Before you try ollies on a halfpipe, make sure you're first able to do them in the street. Also, unlike most grinds and slides, most people find that frontside ollies are easier to learn first. Here's how to do them:

TRICK:

1. Approach the lip at a slight angle, with your knees bent and your weight on the balls of your feet.
2. Just like a street ollie, snap your tail with the ball of your back foot so that it hits the surface of the halfpipe.
3. As the board begins to rise, push the outside edge of your front foot forward to lift your nose and guide the board up into the air.
4. As your board rises into the air, lift your knees up toward your chest.
5. Before you start coming back into the halfpipe, look over your shoulder and focus on your landing spot.
6. Straighten your legs out a bit, landing toward the top of the transition with your knees bent slightly and both of your feet flat on the board.

THE TAIL SLIDE

Once you get the ollie down, you're ready for the most difficult of the intermediate tricks: the tail slide. Again, like the ollie, most people start out doing tail slides in the frontside direction. Before you try this trick, you should be able to do frontside 180 ollies on flat ground. Here's how to do the tail slide:

TRICK:

1. Approach the lip as you would for an ollie, with your front toe hanging slightly off the edge of the board.
2. About two-thirds of the way up the transition, snap a quick little ollie.

3. As you float up towards the lip, quickly rotate your hips and shoulders about 90 degrees.

4. Along with your shoulders and hips, rotate your board so that the nose is facing the opposite wall. Use the ball of your back foot to set your tail on the coping. As your tail is placed firmly on the coping, shift almost all your weight to your back foot.

5. Keeping your knees bent, press down firmly on your tail with your back foot, making it slide smoothly across the lip. Keep your knees bent and stay right on top of your board as you slide.

6. Just before your slide starts to end, drop back into the halfpipe.

CHAPTER FIVE

ADVANCED HALFPIPE TRICKS

A fter mastering some intermediate skills, you are probably ready to get to the next level. Be forewarned: the tricks to follow can be tough, but ultimately they are just variations on beginning and medium-difficulty maneuvers. It takes most skaters a long time to learn and then perfect advanced trick. Don't be discouraged. Instead, persistence, patience, and practice (the three P's), will carry you through.

FRONTSIDE AIRS

An air is basically just a big ollie where you grab the board with your hand.

TRICK:

1. Ride up the transition the same way you would for a frontside ollie, with your weight on the balls of your feet and your knees bent.
2. Press down on your tail with your back foot and snap an ollie (if you're on a vert halfpipe you really don't need to snap your tail because you'll go straight into the air anyway).

3. As your board pops up, lift your knees up toward your body, and reach down to the board with your back hand, and grab a comfortable spot on the deck. Don't try to reach too hard for the board. Just lean back a little, tuck your knees to your chest, let the board float up into your hand, and grab it firmly.
4. As you start to come down, look over your shoulder and spot your landing, just like you would for a frontside ollie.
5. Don't hang on to your grab too long. Let go before you set the board down, and bend your knees a bit for the landing.

FRONTSIDE ROCK-AND-ROLLS

The frontside rock-and-roll is a classic and stylish trick. A frontside rock-and-roll is just like a rock-and roll-to fakie, but instead of coming in backwards you come back in frontside.

TRICK:

1. Roll up the wall at a slight frontside angle, leaning back slightly.
2. Press down on your tail and rest the center of your board on the coping, just like with a rock-and-roll to fakie. Remember to straighten your front leg and press your front wheels down on the deck with your front foot, which will make your back wheels rock up, or lift up off the surface of the halfpipe.
3. As you press your front wheels down on the deck, look directly over your front shoulder at the transition. Arch your back as you look over your shoulder, which will make it easier to come back down the transition.
4. Press down on the tail with the outside edge of your back foot, and lift your front trucks and wheels over the coping. Keep your back knee bent and try bowing your legs out a bit, looking over your shoulder the whole time.

5. Set your front trucks and wheels back on the halfpipe and ride back down the transition.

OLLIE BLUNTS

Also known just as the blunt, this is one of the more technically advanced tricks done on the lip of the halfpipe. A blunt is a trick where you stall with your back truck and tail on the lip, and then ollie back into the halfpipe. Before you try blunts, warm up with a few simple ollie to fakies. Here's how to do them:

TRICK:

1. Ride straight up the transition toward the lip, like you would for a rock-and-roll to fakie. You don't need a lot of speed for this trick. Make sure to have all your weight on the balls of your feet and toes.
2. Just before your front wheels have the chance to hit the coping, press down on your tail with the ball of your back foot.
3. Guide your back wheels up over the coping and onto the deck. Press down firmly on your tail, making your board stall on the coping.
4. Now here's the most difficult part: to get out of the blunt stall position, you have to pop an ollie off the coping. Pop your tail with your back foot, and use the outside edge of your front foot to guide the board up and then back into the halfpipe.
5. As you reenter the halfpipe, put just a little extra weight on your front foot. Once you land, look over your back shoulder at the opposite wall.

FRONTSIDE KICKFLIP

Also known simply as a frontside flip, this is one of the most technically difficult halfpipe tricks (it is almost always done on a

Skate veteran Pete King is shown here executing a frontside air on a ramp.

mini halfpipe that's 6 feet [1.8 m] high or smaller). In order to do this halfpipe trick, you should be really comfortable with ollies on a halfpipe, and you need to have kickflips wired on flatground.

TRICK:

1. Approach the lip at a slight frontside angle, like you would for a frontside ollie.
2. At the top of the half-pipe, pop a good sized ollie.
3. As you ollie, drag the outside edge of you front foot up towards the upper edge of your nose. Use the side of your foot and toe to flick the board one full rotation.
4. After the flick, circle your front foot around the nose of your board, so that the board flips between your legs.
5. Catch the board on your feet and spot your landing over your front shoulder.
6. Bend your knees as you set the board down and ride it out.

backside Any trick in which you turn so that your back faces the coping is considered backside.

bail Falling off your skateboard.

fakie The position when you're riding backwards on the board with your feet in your normal stance

frontside Any trick in which you turn so that your front faces the coping is considered frontside.

grind A trick involving moving the trucks of your board along the edge or top of an object.

halfpipe A ramp with two opposing walls, so that it dips down in the middle and back up on either side.

manual A trick in which you lift up your front trucks and balance on your back wheels while riding. If you balance instead on your front wheels, it's called a nose manual. The manual is also sometimes called a wheelie.

mini-ramp A small halfpipe.

roll-in A smooth convex transition going from a flat platform into a steep transition.

session Whenever a group of skaters get together and ride.

slide These tricks involve moving the bottom of your board along the edge or top of an object.

snake Someone who doesn't wait his or her turn during a session and who takes way too many runs.

stall A trick that involves balancing your board on something for a few seconds without moving forward and then pulling off the object.

switchstance Usually just called "switch." When you do a trick with your feet in the opposite stance that you usually ride.

trucks Also called axles, they are the metal devices that hold your wheels to the board and make it possible to turn.

vert This is a style of skating performed on vert ramps, specifically tricks that are performed while in the air.

vert ramp A specially built halfpipe that curves upward into a vertical incline.

Go Skateboarding Foundation
22431 Antonio Parkway
Rancho Santa Margarita, CA 92688
(949) 455-1112
Website: http://goskateboardingfoundation.org
The Go Skateboarding Foundation provides education, career
    programming, scholarships, and helps fund skateparks.

International Skateboarding Federation (ISF)
P.O. Box 57
Woodward, PA 16882
(814) 883-5635
Website: http://www.internationalskateboardingfederation.com
The International Skateboarding Federation (ISF) is formally orga-
    nized and incorporated to provide direction and governance
    for the sport of skateboarding worldwide.

Skatepark Association of the United States of America (SPAUSA)
2210 Lincoln Boulevard
Venice, CA 90291
Website: http://www.spausa.org
The Skatepark Association of the United States of America
    (SPAUSA) is a nonprofit organization that assists communities
    obtain the resources to build their own skateparks.

Skaters for Public Skateparks
820 North River Street, Loft 206
Portland, OR 97227
Website: http://www.skatepark.org
Skaters for Public Skateparks is a nonprofit advocacy group,
    which provides information to those hoping to finance, build,
    and/or improve their local skateparks and other skating
    venues.

WEBSITES

Because of the changing number of Internet links, Rosen
Publishing has developed an online list of websites related to
the subject of this book. This site is updated regularly. Please
use this link to access this list:

http://www.rosenlinks.com/STT/half

FOR FURTHER READING

Brooke, Michael. *The Concrete Wave: The History of Skateboarding.* Toronto: Warwick Publishing, 1999.

Caitlin, Stephen. *Skateboard Fun.* Mahwah, NJ: Troll Communications, 1988.

Choyce, Lesley. *Skateboard Shakedown.* Halifax, Canada: Formac, 1989.

Christopher, Matt, and Paul Mantell. *Skateboard Renegade.* New York: Little Brown and Company, 2000.

Doeden, Matt. *Skateparks: Grab Your Skateboard.* Mankato, MN: Capstone Press, 2002.

Goodfellow, Evan, and Doug Werner. *Street Skateboarding: Endless Grinds and Slides: An Instructional Look at Curb Tricks.* Chula Vista, CA: Tracks Publishing, 2005.

Hawk, Tony. *Hawk: Occupation: Skateboarder.* New York: Reagan Books, 2000.

Irvine, Alex, and Paul Parker. *So You Think You're a Skateboarder?: 50 Tales from the Street and the Skatepark.* New York, NY: CICO Books, 2014.

Lombard, Kara-Jane (ed.). *Skateboarding: Subcultures, Sites and Shifts* (Routledge Research in Sport, Culture and Society). New York, NY: Routledge, 2015.

Marcus, Ben. *The Skateboard: The Good, the Rad, and the Gnarly.* Minneapolis, MN: MVP Books/Lerner Publishing, 2011.

Michalski, Peter, and Justin Hocking. *Skating Bowls and Pools* (Skateboarding Tips and Tricks). New York, NY: Rosen Publishing, 2016.

Sohn, Emily. *Skateboarding: How it Works* (The Science of Sports – Sports Illustrated for Kids). Mankato, MN: Capstone Publishers, 2010.

Thatcher, Kevin. *Thrasher Presents How to Build Skateboard Halfpipes: Halfpipes, Boxes, Bowls and More.* San Francisco, CA: High Speed Productions, 2001.

Watts, Franklin, and James Nixon. *Skateboarding Champion* (How to Be a Champion). New York, NY: Franklin Watts/ Scholastic, 2015.

Weyland, Jocko. *The Answer Is Never.* New York: Grove Press, 2002.

Wixon, Ben. *Skateboarding: Instruction, Programming and Park Design.* Champaign, IL: Human Kinetics, 2009.

BIBLIOGRAPHY

Badillo, Beal, and Dan Werner. *Skateboarding: Book of Tricks* (Start-Up Sports) Chula Vista, CA: Tracks Publishing, 2003.

Beal, Becky. *Skateboarding: The Ultimate Guide*. Santa Barbara, CA: ABC-CLIO, 2013.

Mullen, Rodney. *The Mutt: How to Skateboard and Not Kill Yourself*. New York, NY: IT Books/HarperCollins, 2004.

Pointx.com. "Contact Us." Retrieved January 24, 2004 (http://www.pointx.com/contact_us.asp).

Skateboard.com. "Camps." Retrieved January 24, 2004 (http://www.skateboard.com/frontside/GetLocal/camps/default.asp).

Skateboarding.com. "This Is the News 5.28.02." Retrieved January 23, 2004 (http://www.skateboarding.com/skate/news/article/0,12364,250225,00.html).

Vansskatecamp.com. "Skate—Summer 2004." Retrieved January 24, 2004 (http://www.vansskatecamp.com/index.htm).

Wixon, Ben. *Skateboarding: Instruction, Programming and Park Design*. Champaign, IL: Human Kinetics, 2009.

INDEX

ABOUT THE AUTHORS

Peter Michalski is a young adult nonfiction author who has penned many instructional titles for teens, covering sports, careers, and health issues.

Justin Hocking lives and skateboards in New York City. He is also an editor of the *book Life and Limb: Skateboarders Write from the Deep End*, published in 2004 by Soft Skull Press.

PHOTO CREDITS

Designer: Michael Moy; Editor: Philip Wolny;
Photo Researcher: Karen Huang and Philip Wolny